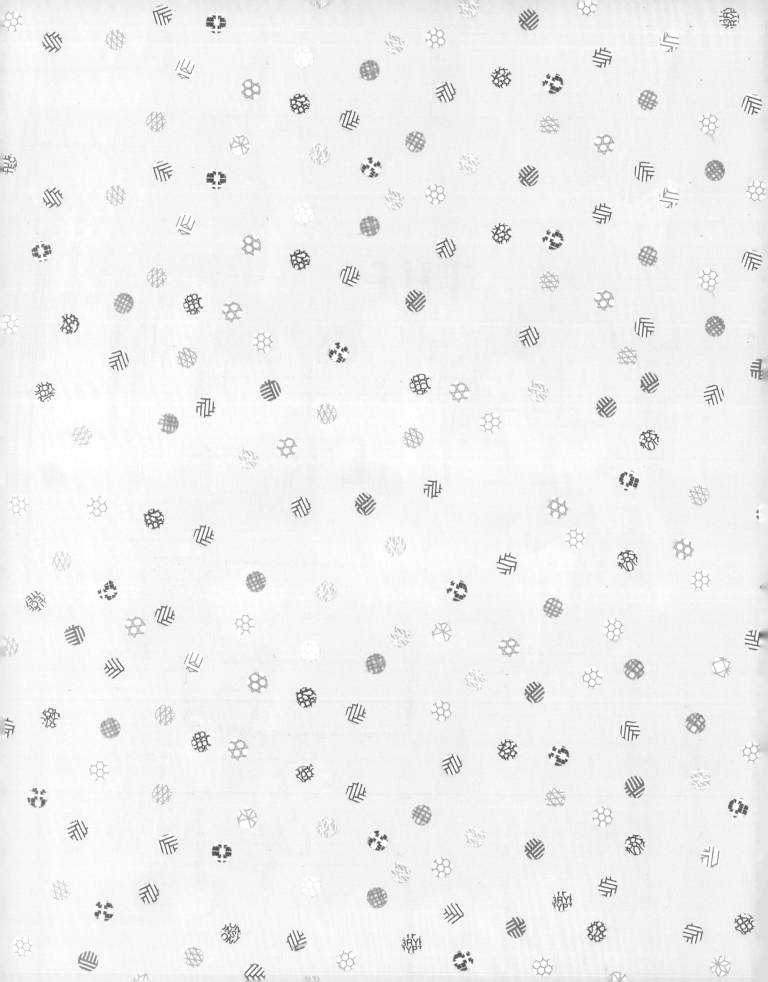

THE THANK YOU LETTER

for Oliver

HOLIDAY HOUSE is registered in the U.S. Patent and Trademark Office.
Printed and bound in February 2019 at Tien Wah Press, Johor Bahru, Johor, Malaysia.
The artwork for this book was created with acrylic paint and collage on paper,
including patterns from the inside of envelopes.
www.holidayhouse.com
First Edition
1 3 5 7 9 10 8 6 4 2
Library of Congress Cataloging-in-Publication Data is available.
ISBN 978-0-8234-4250-8

love from
Jane Cabrera

THE THANK YOU LETTER

Jane Cabrera

Holiday House
New York

Grace's Birthday
was almost here.
She had written a list.

Things I would like for my BIRTHDAY

Puppy →

Robot →

Books on how to build a den. →

sparkly shoes ↓

Pens and paints ←

Magic Wings ←

Tent and Camping things ←

and Lots and Lots of chocolates.

The day of the Party arrived!

There were games and ice cream and presents, and the sun shone all day.

The next day Grace got out
her new pens and pencils
to write Thank You Letters.

Dear Nang and
Granpops,
Thankyou for my
Puppy.
Love Grace
x
← called Bob

(Although she didn't write
that what she really wanted
was a REAL Puppy.)

Dear Taye,
Thankyou for the
magic wings. I have
not tested the
magic yet. love
Grace x

Dear Milly and
Billy,
Thankyou for my
sparkly shoes.
love your favorite
cousin! Grace x

Dear Aunt Mary,
Thankyou for the
gloves. They are a
little too big at
the moment.
Love Grace x

Dear Poppy,
Thankyou for the
soft toy. I have
called it Geoffrey.
Love Grace x

She only stopped for one quick snack.

Dear Mom and Dad
Thankyou for my
fun party and for the
bestest tent ever.
Love Me (Grace)
x x x

Friendly Bear

Bing

pizza and lemonade

Dear Jayla,
Thankyou for the pens
and pencils.
I love them!
Love Grace.
                    X

Dear Noah,
Thankyou for the
most awesome
Robot costume.
Love your sizter
Grace x

But Grace did not stop there.
Next, she wrote a Thank You to her Cat.

A Thank You to the Lady in the thrift store.

A Thank You to her favorite Teacher.

Dear Mr. Jones,
Thank you
for teaching
me my
Letters.
Love Grace
x

A Thank You to her Dog.

Grace even wrote a
Thank You to the Sky!
She put it on a tree, as
high as she could reach.

And still she wrote some more.

Soon Thank You Letters appeared all over town.
They made everyone very happy.

So, one afternoon when Grace
came home from school, she ran up
to her new tent, and . . .

It was full
of LOVE notes.

Love notes EVERYWHERE.

Grace read each and every one.

Of course, she then wrote lots of her own, along with one last special Thank You Letter.